MOON BEACH
Mysteries

D1540325

by
Richard L. Baldwin

Richard L. Baldwin (signature)

Illustrated by Dawn McVay Baumer

©Buttonwood Press 2003

ISBN 0-9660685-9-9

Disclaimer

This set of stories is the product of the imagination of the author. None of the events described in this story occurred. Though settings, buildings, businesses exist, liberties may have been taken as to their actual location and description. This story has no purpose other than to entertain the reader. The names of the Svetnicka family are used with their permission as well as the first names of current employees of Moon Beach Camp. Any other references to people or companies is coincidental.

Published by

Buttonwood Press, LLC
P.O. Box 716
Haslett, Michigan 48840
www.buttonwoodpress.com

Dedication

This book of short stories is dedicated to
Glenn, Adele, Christian, Sophia,
and Luciano Svetnicka

Acknowledgements

This was a fun collection of stories to write. In addition to "listening" to my imagination I also enjoyed working with my editor, Gail Garber, whose suggestions for improvement were appreciated; my proofreader, Joyce Wagner, who mysteriously can find tens of mistakes in a perfect document; my illustrator, Dawn McVay Baumer, whose artistic talent captured the essence of the stories; and finally my typesetter, Marilyn "Sam" Nesbitt, who once again came up with a perfect visual presentation of the stories.

Thanks to the Svetnicka family for allowing me to create some stories around them. Thanks to the Board of Directors of Moon Beach Camp for allowing me to place my stories in their peaceful and homey camp setting. Finally, thanks to my wife, Patty Baldwin, for her suggestions, her support, and her love.

Introduction

The Svetnicka family pulled out of Haslett, Michigan, in early June of 2002 to begin a life of service to others at Moon Beach Camp, a Christian camp in northern Wisconsin. Glenn Svetnicka would become the camp manager. As a good-bye gift I decided to write and dedicate a series of stories to them.

Other Books by Richard L. Baldwin

FICTION

Mysteries (No profanity, suitable for teenagers and adults)

A Lesson Plan for Murder (1998)
ISBN: 0-9660685-0-5 — Buttonwood Press

The Principal Cause of Death (1999)
ISBN: 0-9660685-2-1 — Buttonwood Press

Administration Can Be Murder (2000)
ISBN: 0-9660685-4-8 — Buttonwood Press

Buried Secrets of Bois Blanc: Murder in the Straits of Mackinac (2001)
ISBN: 0-9660685-5-6 — Buttonwood Press

The Searing Mysteries: Three in One (2001)
ISBN: 0-9660685-6-4 — Buttonwood Press

The Marina Murders (2002)
ISBN: 0-9660685-7-2 — Buttonwood Press, LLC

Ghostly Links (2003)
ISBN: 0-9660685-8-0 — Butttonwood Press, LLC

Spiritual

Unity and the Children (2000)
ISBN: 0-9660685-3-X — Buttonwood Press

NON-FICTION

The Piano Recital (1999)
ISBN: 0-9660685-1-3 — Buttonwood Press

A Story to Tell: Special Education in Michigan's Upper Peninsula 1902-1975 (1994)
ISBN: 932212-77-8 — Lake Superior Press

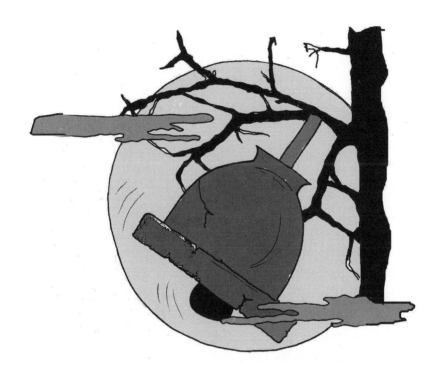

The Masked Ringer
of the Mysterious Bell

The Masked Ringer of the Mysterious Bell

Numerous families with children of all ages were at Moon Beach Camp in northern Wisconsin for fun and sun and a change of pace from hectic lives back home. They wanted to be cared for so that, to use a play on words, they wouldn't have a care in the world. But, little did they know that the quiet and peaceful atmosphere of Moon Beach Camp was often disturbed by the clanging of a bell. There was no bell tower. There was no place for miles around where a bell could be found. There was also the rumor of a ghost.

Most people could let the bell toll and simply ignore it, but these Moon Beach campers would settle for nothing less than an explanation. Back home, bells rang because someone pulled a rope or activated an electric signal. To this group, the unexplained ringing of the bell at Moon Beach Camp must be explained.

Solving this mystery became an obsession with the teens attending the week-long camp.

At first, it sounded like a simple problem. All one needed to do was follow his God-given sense of hearing and go in the direction of the sound until the source could be found. The teens decided to form a search party the next time they heard the bell. The sound seemed to come from north of the camp where there were no cottages, camps or any evidence of humans living in the area.

When the campers heard the bell the next evening, they gathered and began to walk toward the source of the sound with powerful flashlights leading the way. Although they searched for over an hour no bell was ever found and the sound seemed non-existent once they got to the area where it seemed the bell would be, where the sound was the loudest.

When Glenn, the camp manager, heard the bell after he and his family came to the camp, he asked neighbors in the area if they had ever heard the strange bell.  They had for many years and offered two explanations. The first was that the bell called the children for dinner many years ago when a family lived in a cottage in the area. The mother of the children died tragically and the older children pitched in and helped the father raise the youngsters and they managed to get along.

The story goes that once in awhile just before dinner, the bell would ring and when the children looked outside they could not see anyone. They figured it was their mother trying to tell them that she was in Heaven and not to worry. Some people still believe the bell is rung by the mother of those children.

The second theory was that the bell rings whenever something filled with love happens. This theory came forth because on more than one occasion, people heard the bell right after getting some good news like a marriage or the birth of a child. This explained the lack of regularity of the bell, but who rang it, and why was it being rung?

Glenn believed the teens were spending far too much mental energy with this bell and their obsession was robbing them of a summer camping experience. He tried to divert the attention of the teens to activities such as swimming, crafts, spiritual reflection, hiking, boating, and other outdoor events that campers long to do in the winter months when northern Wisconsin is frozen from the famous Door County to the Minnesota border. As hard as Glenn tried to get attention off the bell, the more determined this group of teens became to solving the Mysterious Bell at Moon Beach Camp.

The evening campfire, usually a time for guitars, songs and S'mores, was now an intense planning session to solve the unexplainable. The group, five in number, chose a leader and wrote out clues and steps they would take to try and unravel the mystery. The leader was Sam Nesbitt, a freshman at the University of Wisconsin at Madison; his sister Dawn, who was a high school senior in Appleton; Gail Garber, the daughter of the family camp leader; Jerry Wagner, a worker who assisted the camp's maintenance man; and John Zink, a teen who came to Moon Beach intent on experiencing a spiritual retreat.

Sam suggested that they record the bell ringing so that an analysis of the sound could be conducted. It was important to determine if the sound was really a ringing bell. Glenn had a recorder in his office. It wasn't of high quality, but it was better than nothing and might do the trick.

The remainder of the time around the campfire was spent thinking of clues and coming up with theories to explain this mystery. Tim was sure the bell was not really a bell but only a sound that over the water increased in volume; and if they could only find the source, it would be something simple and easily explained. On the other end of the continuum, Gail was sure the sound was caused by some aliens who had come to earth and used the bell to scare people away so they would not be discovered.

As the evening grew late, talk around the fire had dwindled. In an instant, the fire went out as quickly and completely as blowing out a match. Everyone was stunned at suddenly being thrust into total darkness.

Glenn tried to assure everyone that all was well. "I'm sure there is an explanation for this. Right now, let's just get back to camp. Line up, put your right hand on the shoulder of the person in front of you and follow me. I know the path back to the lodge and with a little moonlight to show the way, we'll get back safely."

Sam got everyone's attention when he said, "Shhh, hear that? The bell!" The darkness engulfed them and they could hear the eerie sound of the distant bell.

While the group of six walked single file back to the lodge with Glenn in the lead, each person contemplated the fire and

how it could be extinguished without anyone doing anything to it and with no change in weather. Everyone in line was calm. Jerry interrupted the quiet walk when he said in a loud whisper, "I think Moon Beach Camp is inhabited by ghosts." "I agree. That can be the only explanation!" Gail replied. Glenn, sensing potential panic, jumped in, "Let's not get all worked up here. I'm sure there's a simple explanation for the fire going out. Nobody was threatened. We didn't see or hear anything that would be disturbing. We are almost to the lodge. Stay calm and all will be well."

"But we heard THE BELL," Dawn said. "Maybe the bell rings before something terrible happens."

"There goes your imagination," Glenn said, hoping people would not panic. "Stay calm. All is well."

Glenn's reassuring manner worked as the people believed him and continued their slow but sure hike to the lodge. The lights in the lodge were a welcome sight for had the lodge been dark, the campers would have pretty much lost it. Vivid imaginations would replace reality and Glenn might have pure panic going from Vesper Point to the lodge.

Once back at the lodge, Glenn suggested folks get a snack in the kitchen and then head to their cabins for a good night's sleep. Tomorrow would be another day and the amateur detectives could once again resume their quest for a full explanation to the mysterious bell, as well as fires that extinguish without any intervention by people or elements.

"This group is determined. Other groups talk about it and then get on with the camping experience, but this small group of teenagers is obsessed with the mystery," Glenn said to his wife Adele when he got home.

Before Glenn and Adele went to bed, Glenn decided to watch the news. It was his one and only link to the world, a crazy world that he left behind when he took the job to manage the

7

camp. In spite of this strange bell and the stresses of being responsible for hundreds of people, he couldn't imagine going back to the fast-paced life outside the gates of Moon Beach. Watching the news not only allowed him to be grateful for the camp's peaceful aura, but also linked him to what everyone else in the world was finding important.

As soon as he turned on the television he heard, "We want to give you the latest in a mystery currently taking place in northern Wisconsin. Our correspondent is Wesley Leonard. Wes, what can you tell us?"

"Thanks, Brad. The best word I can use to describe it is, chaotic. Rumors of aliens are rampant in northern rural Wisconsin. The phone calls are coming in one after the other and each call is a report of something strange happening, something that cannot be explained."

"Les, are you hearing anything from beyond the area of rural Wisconsin? Any reports from Michigan, the Upper Peninsula, or Minnesota for example?"

"No, nothing from beyond about a twenty square mile area, I'd say."

"Any clue why all of this unexplained activity is limited to this area?"

"No, I've learned that one of Rhinelander's oldest citizens said he thinks it has something to do with a bell at a church camp."

"You mean the source of all of this craziness is a church camp?" Brad asked.

"I can't confirm anything because the camp is unknown and we're not even sure of the name of the place, Brad. Apparently, some think this is due to disturbed spirits."

"Really? Disturbed spirits?" Brad responded with astonishment.

"Apparently whenever humans try to get nosy and explain the unexplainable, the forces, whatever that means, are angered and sort of go loony for awhile. We are thinking that either this church camp is the central point for the aliens or people at the camp are getting too nosy for their own good and are the reason for all of this chaos. That's all I have for now. Back to you, Brad."

To say that Glenn had a problem was to put it mildly. All he came to Moon Beach for was to manage a wonderful peaceful camp in northern Wisconsin; and now, maybe because this group of campers was taking the mystery a bit seriously, the camp and all the people currently on the premises might be catapulted into the national media. His leadership skills were about to be tested in a rather unique way. He gave Adele a hug and looked Heavenward and let out a sigh. The next day or perhaps before the sun rose, Moon Beach Camp could be the center of the universe, being served its fifteen minutes of fame.

Glenn's first instincts were to call the Chairman of the Board of Directors for the camp. He needed to alert him to what was happening and get his support for any decisions that needed to be made to bring some calm to a potentially explosive situation. The chairman appreciated the heads up and gave Glenn his full support for handling the crisis.

After consulting with his earthly boss, Glenn turned to his Heavenly Boss. He knew he was not alone and that the Holy Spirit was constant and always with him. He felt confident that he would be given the right thing to say and do given the situations that came to him.

It was obvious that trying to keep people out or to try and hide something would only fan the fires of curiosity. Glenn also knew that he needed everyone's help and that a unified effort by those at Moon Beach Camp would be best. He awakened all the campers and called for a meeting in the lodge. People were dazed and some thought this was some type of practical camp joke when Glenn told them of the news report and what the reporters had said.

It was about two in the morning when Glenn briefed all present that the camp may soon be descended upon like hawks circling fresh road kill. Being a Christian camp, he led the group in a prayer that common sense would prevail and that a logical explanation would be the result of all the attention that could be brought to the camp.

John had a cell phone and called a good friend to find out what was being said in the media. What John learned was shared with others and soon, each camper had full knowledge of what was happening within and outside of the twenty square miles of which they were smack dab in the middle.

"Listen," Dawn said. Instantly, all stopped talking or moving. The silence that engulfed everyone allowed the faint sound of a bell to be heard and to let everyone know that the mysterious sound was active once again.

"If we could only solve the mystery, we'd be able to bring calm to everyone and explain the craziness that's going on," Jerry said. All present nodded.

All of a sudden there was a crashing sound that seemed to come from the kitchen. It sounded like the huge pots and pans suspended from a ceiling rack came crashing to the ground. Dawn was closest to the kitchen. She pushed open the door to see what had happened when she was blinded by a bright light. She immediately reached up to cover her eyes and fell backward as if a great wave of energy pushed her away from the door.

Some of the campers went to Dawn's aid while Glenn cautiously approached the kitchen door to open it again while being careful not to look inside. As the door opened, there was no flash of light. Glenn looked in and saw a perfectly normal kitchen. Nothing had fallen and nothing was out of place. He went in and checked the food storage area and then out back thinking an animal had gotten into the garbage cans, but all was in order. There was no explanation for the sound and the blinding flash of light.

Someone noticed that the framed picture of Jesus, normally hanging above the entrance to the dining room, was missing. Everyone's attention was directed to the blank wall. The bell, the fire going out with no explanation, the missing picture of Jesus, and the crash of pots and pans along with the bright flash of light were adding up to a lot of unexplained occurrences that quite frankly had people worried and concerned.

Dawn quickly regained her sight and had just a slight headache. Glenn began to imagine what might happen if all of this escalated. His camp would be the center of a lot of attention. He would probably get a call from Jay Leno and David Letterman. He soon might be talking to Katie Couric and Matt Lauer. *USA Today* and *People* magazine would be two of many newspapers and magazines wanting to know what was going on. Interested psychologists around the world would be coming to Moon Beach Camp to study the paranormal, write stories, and conduct experiments. This would put Moon Beach Camp on the map, not as a Christian retreat center where souls can be renewed to serve the Lord, but a place full of mysterious happenings. Shaking himself out of this train of thought, Glenn decided to turn Heavenward for help.

Glenn believed in the power of prayer. He asked all the campers to join him in prayer and to ask for direction on how best to handle the attention that was moving toward the camp, getting closer with each minute.

The silence of prayerful souls was interrupted when John suggested that they simulate the mystery as a means of explaining it.

"What do you mean?" Sam asked.

"I mean, I think we get the bell that calls us to dinner and we take it into the woods and ring it on occasion."

"I don't see where you are going with this, John," Glenn said, scratching his head.

"When the media and the law enforcement get here, we simply express surprise at all the commotion because the campers are just ringing a bell. What's so loony about that?" John asked. "The bell is a reminder of that line in Dunne's poem, '...do not ask for whom the bell tolls, it tolls for thee.' We ring it on occasion to remind ourselves that we need each other in all that we do because we're all connected."

"Hmm, interesting," Glenn said. "But, how do we explain the fire going out and the flash of light and sound in the kitchen?"

"We don't because we can't," John replied. "We need to accept the fact that some things cannot be explained or understood. We have to accept some mysteries in life."

"I see where you are going, but the plan is deceitful," Glenn said. "We are continuing the confusion and passing on information that does not help solve the mystery."

"Glenn's right," Sam said.

"Listen, there is the bell again," Dawn said.

"I suggest we take our flashlights and fan out while moving toward the bell," Sam suggested. "We keep going in the direction of the sound and if we stay about 10 yards or so apart, we've got to find it."

The campers did as Sam suggested. They knew they were making some progress because the sound was getting louder. The basics of physics told the campers that the bell couldn't be far away as sound only travels so far. The source would be evident soon.

It was nearing 3:30 in the morning when the bell stopped, but one of the campers suggested that they move forward anyway. That decision was pivotal because about five minutes later, Jerry tripped and the flashlight flew out of his hand as he tumbled forward. A cry for help brought a few campers to Jerry's side. The flashlight was positioned so that the beam of light was pointed upward into a tree. Thankfully, Gail looked up before taking the flashlight from the ground and in looking up she saw two huge raccoons and an old bell.

After being sure that Jerry's ankle was not sprained or broken, the campers shined their lights on the raccoons high in the tree and to their surprise, they saw an old dinner bell wedged between a few large branches. It seemed that the raccoons treated the bell as a toy. How the bell got up in the tree remained a mystery but no longer were people in the dark about the sound of the bell.

Gail believed that years ago, some campers stole the bell and put it high in a tree as a prank. Over time the event was forgotten. Sam suggested that whenever people came close, the raccoons would either leave the tree or stop playing with the bell. If he were right, it would explain why the source of the sound could never be identified and why the bell only rang sometimes.

Thankfully, Dawn had brought a digital camera along and took photos of the discovery. The photos would offer instant proof that the mystery had been solved. The campers returned to the lodge with each taking a turn at helping Jerry hobble along. They decided, however, to leave the bell up in the tree.

Once the campers returned to the lodge, Glenn's son Christian had the solution to the fire going out. Christian had discovered that the wood used for the fire had been standing on end in several inches of water from a week of steady rain. As the fire burned down to the water-logged wood, it lost the oxygen supply necessary for a fire to burn and went out.

Now, all that was left to explain was the crashing sound and flash of light in the kitchen. If this could be explained, all of the strange occurrences at the Moon Beach Camp would have logical explanations. That explanation came when the daughter of one of the adult campers admitted to working on a camp story for a creative writing project. She dropped a few pans and then when someone came into the kitchen a camera flash would go off a foot or two from the face of the investigating party. The prankster then put the pans back and left through the back door.

"Looks like we've spent a lot of time and energy on this mystery to find out that we were dealing with raccoons who loved a bell and an inconsiderate youngster using some bad judgment for an essay," Adele said.

"That's about it," Glenn said, while heaving a sigh. "I feel a let down. I sort of liked our friendly ghost at Moon Beach; I'm sorry to learn the truth, to be honest."

"Yeah, I know what you mean. Every camp needs a friendly ghost."

"I wonder what all the commotion was down around Rhinelander."

"You should call the sheriff," Adele suggested. "See what he has to say."

Glenn called the sheriff early the next morning. "What can you tell me about the craziness around Rhinelander last night?"

"Mass hysteria, Glenn. Strange things happened in a few towns about the same time and the people panicked. It was all related to power outages."

"That's good to hear. What was the rumor about a church camp?"

"It wasn't Moon Beach. It was camp south of Eagle River. Apparently, some kids called home on cell phones telling parents about ghosts. The kids did it as a prank and got a pretty stern talking to by the camp director. So, put it all together and you got people going loony on a hot summer night. All is OK now."

"That's good to hear," replied Glenn. "I thought we'd be right in the middle of a huge media circus."

"You've been spared, Glenn. Go back to bed if you can and then enjoy another beautiful day in northern Wisconsin."

The next morning, the teens were walking around like zombies. The excitement plus practically no sleep left all in a stupor. Half asleep they ate pancakes and bacon and felt quite satisfied in having solved the Case of The Masked Ringer of the Mysterious Bell at Moon Beach Camp.

The End

The Case of
the Missing Canoes

The Case of the Missing Canoes

"Christian, please go to the waterfront and count the canoes on the racks," Glenn Svetnicka, the manager of Moon Beach Camp, said shortly after sunrise.

"Sure, Dad," Christian said. Christian was thirteen years old, an avid reader, and a young boy who dreamed of becoming a detective. "How many are supposed to be there?"

"We have a baker's dozen and hopefully not an unlucky 13."

"I'll be back with a report."

"Thanks, son."

Christian walked out into the cool July morning. The grass was still covered with dew and he soon found his toes wet as he walked quickly toward the waterfront. He was enjoying the summer break from school. The couple of months would give Christian time to read a lot of mysteries and maybe to write one. He loved the suspense and detective work in mysteries. Once in awhile he could solve the case before the author revealed the solution, but that was rare. Most of the time he missed a clue that would have helped him solve it. Christian often dreamed of having his own case to solve and then he would write about it and maybe even publish his own book.

Christian could see the silver canoes with "Moon Beach Camp" painted on the side. As he got closer he could see the state-issued identification numbers on the front of the canoes. He began to count the boats resting on racks. When Christian got to nine he quickly added the three on the top row and knew that one was missing. He looked out into the lake and in the brush around the canoeing area but did not see the 13th canoe.

Christian went up to the tag board and saw 13 tags. He counted the paddles and a perfect 26 paddles were hanging from a rack behind the canoes. Hmmm, Dad won't like this, he thought. Christian ran back to the camp manager's home, known to all as The White House, pushed open the screen door, and began to give his report. "I only counted 12, Dad."

"You sure? Did you double count?"

"Yeah, I counted three or four times to make sure. I looked out in the lake and around in the bushes, but I didn't see one. The tags are on the hooks and all the paddles are there."

"That's strange."

"Why did you ask me to check, Dad? Did you suspect one had been stolen?"

"Just had a feeling."

"A feeling? Did you hear a noise down there in the night? Or see something?" Christian asked.

"No, like I said, I just had a feeling. Let's go to the lodge for breakfast. I'll announce that a canoe is missing and see if anyone knows anything. Could be something innocent. On the other hand, we could have a thief inside or outside the camp."

Christian rubbed his hands together thinking he finally would have his case to solve. Having a thief around was troubling, but the chance to solve a real crime was a perfect way to spend his vacation. Christian said he'd be at the lodge in a few minutes. He went back to the waterfront and began to look for clues. There were many footprints and shoeprints, but it would be difficult, if not impossible, to determine which of the prints belonged to a thief.

The missing canoe was canoe #9. That in itself meant nothing, but Christian noted it none the less. He looked at the beach and saw markings in the wet sand that could have been the canoe being pushed into the lake or maybe it was the last canoe to be dragged to shore for placement on the rack. He wasn't able to find anything that would be helpful. The boat area at the waterfront looked very normal.

As Christian walked to the lodge for breakfast he thought to himself, *If someone were going to steal a canoe, why wouldn't they take a couple of paddles? Maybe they brought their own.*

Fearing the worst, Glenn checked with each counselor to be assured that all campers were accounted for. Thankfully, the check showed all registered campers present. That was a relief. At the same time, Glenn mentioned to each counselor that the camp was missing a canoe and asked if they had any idea where it might be or if they recalled any camper leaving the cabin for a period of time in the night. He heard nothing that would help him.

During a breakfast of pancakes and bacon Glenn decided not to announce the missing canoe because he thought that some campers might be worried about the safety of their belongings. *I'll wait before making an announcement - maybe we can explain this in time,* thought Glenn.

Christian picked at his food because his mind was on a strategy for solving the case of the missing canoe. He couldn't wait to get to work. His first effort was to contact the nearby

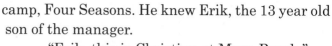

camp, Four Seasons. He knew Erik, the 13 year old son of the manager.

"Erik, this is Christian at Moon Beach."

"Hey. What's on your mind?"

"You got all of your canoes?"

"All of our what?"

"Canoes."

"Why?"

"Just curious. Would you see if they're all there and if not, give me a call, OK?"

Erik went to the waterfront and counted the canoes. One was missing. Erik told his mother and then called Christian.

"One is missing. Did your campers steal it?" Erik asked. His observation was legit because it seemed that each summer there were always a couple of inter-camp pranks.

"Nope. Looks like we've got a canoe thief in these parts."

"Hmmm, does the thief take the paddles too?"

"Didn't take any of our paddles," Christian said. "You might want to check yours."

Christian also decided to take a canoe out on the lake and look around. Sometimes a canoe is not brought up far enough onto shore and it floats away at the mercy of the wind. He told his dad his plan, took a paddle and left the waterfront. He decided to paddle over to Four Seasons Camp to talk to Erik.

Christian learned that all of the paddles were at Four Seasons.

"Hmmm, this doesn't make sense, Erik."

"I don't think we've got a thief. If we did the guy would take a lot more than one and he'd take the paddles and life preservers."

"I agree, but where are the canoes?" Christian asked.

"I don't know. Have fun trying to solve it."

"I'll try. By the way, what was the number on your boat that's missing?" Christian asked.

"The state ID number?" Erik asked.

"No, don't you have a number on your boats, like 5 or 6?"

"Yeah, but I don't know which one is missing. I'll find out and give you a call."

"Thanks."

Christian got back into his canoe and headed for Moon Beach Camp. As he moved through the water, skillfully guiding the canoe in a perfectly straight line, he would often look to shore to see if he could see a canoe or anything suspicious. He didn't see anything but the shoreline, trees, bushes, and beach grass.

When Christian got back to camp, his dad told him that Erik had called and said that the missing canoe was number 5. "I guess that's supposed to mean something?"

"No, not right now anyway. The Four Seasons Camp is missing a canoe, too, Dad. I was trying to see if we were the only camp hit with the theft."

"Later today I plan to take the motorboat around the lake to see if I can find the canoe. I can't imagine anyone would take it off the lake. I mean there are a lot of canoes between our camp and the public access site. Nobody would come all the way to Moon Beach to take one canoe."

"I agree. I'd like to go with you, Dad."

"OK, I've got some chores to do. We'll go after lunch."

Christian's next move was to talk with the camper who had the #9 canoe the day before it was found missing. The records at the waterfront showed that the canoe had been signed out to Connie and Hugh. He saw Connie walking to her cabin and called to her.

"Connie, can I talk to you?"

"Hi, Christian. Sure."

"You and Hugh took out the number 9 canoe yesterday. Right?"

"I guess so. They all look alike to me."

"Well, that canoe is missing and I'm curious if you might have any idea where it might be."

"You think I took it?"

"Oh, no. But, you may have seen someone watching our camp from out in the lake, or someone might have talked to you about the canoe."

"I don't think I can help. I didn't see anyone and I don't think Hugh did either."

"You two went out for a ride, I take it?"

"Yeah. Hugh wanted to fish a little."

"Catch anything?"

"He did, a big pike actually. He threw it back, but it was huge," Connie said and then she started to laugh.

"What's so funny about catching a fish?" Christian asked.

"I told him he should do something so he wouldn't forget where the fish was. He said he would put a mark on the canoe and then he'd remember," Connie said, still chuckling.

"I don't get it. What's so funny?"

"Oh, that joke is so old, Christian. How could he mark the canoe and know where the fish was? You don't get it?"

"Oh, I get it. I got it when you told me. I just don't see what's so funny." Christian was jotting down what Connie was saying. "Thanks, Connie. I need to find Hugh."

"Good luck solving your case."

Christian looked at the schedule of camper activities on the community board. He saw that Hugh would be on the softball field. He went there and asked the sports counselor if he could talk to Hugh. He was called in from the outfield and walked up to Christian.

"I understand that you caught a pike yesterday in canoe number 9."

"Yeah. Why?"

"Connie said you were going to mark the canoe so you'd know where the fish was."

"OK. I confess. I took my jackknife and etched a fish into the side of the canoe. Connie was laughing her head off when I said I would put a mark on the canoe to remind me where I caught the fish."

"Etched a fish?"

"Yeah, you know, those Christian fish symbols you see on the back of cars. I think you have one on the back of your van."

"Yes, we do. On which side of the canoe did you etch the fish? And, how big was the etching?" Christian asked.

"It was on the right side and it was about an inch or two is all."

"You were sitting in the back of the canoe, right?"

"Yes."

"Thanks, Hugh. You may have given me the best clue yet in solving this case."

"You mean I'm not in trouble?"

"Not with me. You are probably going to be a hero when this is all over."

"Cool."

Christian knew that if the canoe was stolen, the state ID numbers would be removed but an etching into an aluminum canoe would be permanent.

After lunch, Christian took his binoculars and his notebook and met his dad at the camp manager's dock. Normally, Christian would have wanted to drive the boat, but today he was going to give all of his attention to the shoreline, looking as far into the brush as he could. Father and son went all around the lake and found no evidence of a canoe. It seemed to be a wasted trip since nothing was found. But, for Christian it meant that he could check off an inspection of the area as a completed task in trying to find the canoe.

It was when Christian was walking to his house after tying up the motorboat that a thought struck him, *Why am I thinking the canoe was taken out into the water. If a paddle wasn't stolen, the canoe was probably taken to the road, loaded onto a truck or a trailer and driven away.*

"I'll be back, Dad. I want to keep looking for the number 9 canoe."

"This mystery has you in its grip, doesn't it, son?"

"I'm going to solve it, Dad. This is my first real case."

"I'll bet you will."

"Have you called the sheriff yet?" Christian asked.

"No, I probably should, but I want to see if you can solve it first. I am not too excited about having police cars around here. It gets the campers upset and they are wild enough as it is. I really would appreciate your solving this case for us."

Christian went to the canoe storage area at the waterfront and instead of focusing on the water, turned inland and started to go in a direction a thief would travel if he was going to the road. He did see some trampling and some footprints, but nothing he could attribute to thieves as opposed to campers collecting fireflies or butterflies or simply walking off the paths going to and from camp activities.

Christian's mom Adele was going into town to do some shopping. "I'm going to town. Do you want to go, Christian?"

"No, I think, I'll stay... wait a minute, I'll change my mind and go."

"Ok, tell your brother to get in the car and make sure your sister is with your dad."

"All set, Mom, let's go."

On the way into town, Christian saw a sign. It read, "Canoe Trips—Sign Up Now—River Fun in Northern Wisconsin. Call 776-5555 for Reservations!"

"Is that sign new?" Christian asked.

"I have no idea. It does look like a new sign though."

"I think so, too." Christian took out his notebook and noted the number and the wording on the sign.

While Adele went in Twig's grocery store with his 8-year-old brother Luciano, Christian went to the pay phone. He took thirty-five cents from his front pocket and called the number of the canoe livery.

"River Trips. Don speaking."

"I'm interested in learning more about your trips. Some friends and I want to do some camping."

"Sure. You want information on the phone or can you come over?"

"I'd like to come over. I want to see your canoes and a map of your river routes."

"Sure. We're four miles west of town on the Wisconsin River. You'll see our sign about a half mile before the bridge."

"Thanks. I'll stop by."

Adele came out of Twig's pushing a cart filled with bags of groceries. Luciano was following her, carrying a jug of milk.

"Mom, can you take me west of town a bit?"

"Not today. We've got to get home. I've got milk, ice cream, and some other perishables. Where do you want to go?"

"I want to go to that canoe place we saw advertised on a sign coming into town."

"Another time. I've got to get this food home and into the freezer.

Christian knew that his next step in solving the crime was going to this River Trip place and he'd have to get there one way or another.

Christian called Erik at Four Seasons Camp when he got back from shopping and putting away some groceries for his mother. "Erik, Christian here. Can you tell me anything about the canoe that's missing at your camp?"

"Tell you anything about it? What do you mean?"

"I mean, did it have any markings on it? Did it have any patches or scrapes?"

"It had some broken straps on the seat. All of our canoes have some broken straps in the seat webbing. Dad says we're not going to get any repairs till the camp season is over."

"Every canoe has some straps that are broken?"

"I think so."

"What color are the straps?"

"Green. It matches the color of our Four Seasons Camp logo on the side."

"Thanks, Eric."

"Sure. You about to solve this thing?"

"I'm working on it. I've got a lead but it might go nowhere. I'll let you know if I solve it."

"**D**ad, I need to go into town," Christian said as his father was signing an invoice for Phil, a truck driver who brought food to the camp.

"Mom went into town earlier, son. No sense making two trips a day."

"I'm going to town from here, Glenn, and in a couple of hours, I'm coming back this way; I could take him," Phil offered.

"That would be OK, I guess."

"Thanks, Dad."

Christian got his camera, notebook, and his ball cap, and he was ready to once again resume his quest to solve the mystery.

Riding in a semi was a lot of fun. It seemed like he was sitting two stories up in a building looking down at the road flying under him. Phil would let him blow the horn when kids gave him the signal to toot.

"What do you need in town, Christian?"

"I don't need anything in town. I want to go to a canoe place about 5 miles west of town."

"How are you going to get there?"

"I don't know. I'll figure it out. Maybe I can convince some kid to let me borrow his bike."

"Are you kidding me? Nobody is going to let you do that. You are an honest kid, Christian, but nobody would let you ride away on their bike. You are pretty naïve to think so, pal."

"Maybe I'll hitchhike then."

"No way. I told your dad I'd bring you to town and bring you back. I'm not going to allow you out of my sight, young man."

"Hey, I'm 13. I can take care of myself."

"You're right. You probably can, but I'm not getting in trouble."

"It will be a wasted trip then. I don't need anything from town. I'll just ride along."

"You told your dad you needed to go to town. I wouldn't get in the habit of telling him lies, young man. A 13-year-old better be figuring out what's honest and abiding by it."

"I did need to go to town. I've got to get to town to get to where I need to go, the canoe place."

"Well, you've got a point there. I'm ahead of schedule. I'll drive you out there. You going to be long?"

"Ten minutes max."

"OK, I can spare that."

"Thanks, Phil. I'll return the favor someday. You can count on it."

Once Phil pulled into the city limits, he asked Christian, "Ok, where is this place you need to go?"

"It's five miles west of town. Take the main road, I guess."

The semi left the city limits and headed for the canoe livery.

"What are you doing going to a canoe place?" Phil asked. "You've got a dozen or so back at the camp."

"Yeah, but I'm trying to solve a crime and I've got a lead that I need to check out."

"Oh, great. Now, I'm taking you someplace where you could get hurt. This is the last time I'm volunteering to take you somewhere."

"I'm just going to look around. I'll be in view the whole time."

"You got that right!"

Phil pulled up to the canoe place and parked off the side of the road before the bridge over the river. Christian said, "I'll be right back," and off he went with camera and notebook. He walked right to a rack of canoes. There had to be about 25, all ready to be pulled by a pickup.

"What can I do for you, young man?" Christian heard from behind him.

"Just looking at your canoes is all."

"You thinking of taking a canoe trip?"

"Might. But my dad is pretty picky about canoes. He only wants the best. They got to be new, good seat webbing and as sturdy as they come."

"We got new canoes and we got used canoes. We can take care of you."

"Good. I'm just checking the equipment out for my dad. Give me a flyer if you've got one. My dad doesn't like high prices, though."

"Our family rates are very good," the man replied. "Is that your dad up there in the semi?"

"Naw, he's a friend who takes me on his route once in awhile. I asked him to stop so I could check your place out."

"I'll get you a flyer to give to your folks."

"Before you do that, where are your used canoes? We might take one of them if they're in good shape."

"Over there in the back."

While the man went into the office, Christian went to the used canoes and inspected them. They looked to be recently painted. He couldn't tell if the names of the two camps were under the coat of paint. Christian then looked at the seats and noticed that the webbing was green and some of the straps were broken. The man returned.

"These seats aren't good."

"Yeah, I know. As I said, these are used canoes. We get big groups in here and we need plenty of canoes. We'll get them fixed in time."

"Where did you get these used canoes?" Christian asked, looking the man in the eye.

"Well, where we buy our canoes is not your business."

"Oh, sure. I was just asking in case we wanted to buy a used canoe. I guess I'll take that flyer and be on my way. Thanks."

"Sure. Hope you and your family take one of our river trips."

Christian walked to the semi and got in. Phil started the truck, turned it around and the two headed back to town and then after a delivery, back toward the camp.

"Solve it?" Phil asked.

"Nope."

"A waste of time?"

"Nope. The canoes have new paint. I wasn't able to see anything helpful, but I'm suspicious of the guy, I'll tell you that."

"You think the guy's a thief?" Phil asked.

"Well, yeah, it's a new canoe business. There are canoes missing at camps and they have used canoes on the racks with green web seating like at Four Seasons, and all the used canoes have fresh paint."

"Sounds to me like you've got nothing to take to the police."

"Right. Not yet, anyway." The two went down the highway, tooting their horn for the kids along the way.

Once back at the camp, Christian reported to his dad.

"I've got a good suspect, Dad, but not enough evidence to accuse him of stealing our canoe."

"You won't want to hear this, but we had another canoe taken, right in broad daylight."

"You're kidding me?"

"I wish I were. I asked the canoe instructor to keep track of the numbers and while we were all at lunch we went from twelve canoes to eleven."

Christian ran to the phone and called Erik. "We've been hit again. Have you guys got all of your canoes?"

"I'll go check. I can count them from our front window. Hang on." Erik picked up his binoculars and looked out their front window.

"We're one short."

"You sure?"

"Yup, the campers are resting after lunch. The waterfront is closed."

"Thanks, Erik. Do you want to go with me? Dad and I are going to town to hopefully wrap up this case."

"Yeah, I'll ask my mom and be right over."

Christian reported to his dad. "Erik says that they've lost a canoe, too."

"We've got to take some action now. I've got to call the sheriff."

"Dad, ask the sheriff to follow us to that new canoe place west of town. I think our canoes are there."

"You sure, son? It will be embarrassing to accuse someone and have the person be innocent."

"If we find what I think we'll find, they're the thieves."

"Ok, Christian. I'm going to trust you."

"Thanks, Dad. Erik is going with us. He can identify any canoes from Four Seasons."

"Ok. I'm ready to go. Is he on his way?"

"He had to ask his mom and then he's coming over."

Glenn called the sheriff and told the dispatcher about the missing canoes and that he would like to talk to them about a possible suspect. The police told him to come to the Department to tell them what he knew. Glenn, Christian, and Erik drove to town. Christian's heart was beating like crazy. If he were right, he'd have his first case solved. If he were wrong, it would embarrass him, his dad, and his friend.

The three talked to the police telling them what they knew and suspected. The sheriff suggested they all go to the canoe place and see what they could learn.

The sheriff's car pulled up, the sheriff and Christian got out of his cruiser while Glenn and Erik remained in the vehicle.

"Hello, Sheriff. What brings you to River Tours?"

"I have a few questions for you."

"Sure, Sheriff. Have people been speeding on the river in our canoes?" the owner asked, trying to make light of the situation.

"Nothing like that. I need to see the receipts for your canoe purchases."

"Come on into our office. I'll get them. What's the problem?"

"We've had some canoes stolen at some local camps so we're checking places where canoes are used to see if we can locate them."

"You're accusing me of stealing canoes from some camps?"

"No, just asking for your proof of purchase."

"Here is the receipt for our 20 new canoes. We bought these about two weeks ago from a place down in Rhinelander." The officer looked at the receipt and said, "Looks legit. You got receipts for your used canoes?"

"Let's see. They should be in this drawer here. Here we go."

The sheriff took about five receipts and saw that the canoe livery had taken delivery of two canoes on four different occasions from a company called, Northern Wisconsin Used Sports Equipment.

"Where is this business?"

"You know, I don't know. A guy comes by in a pickup and asks if I need to buy any used canoes. I don't know where he's from and don't care. I get the canoes I need and he gets paid. If they're hot, I didn't know about it."

"This receipt has no address or phone number," the sheriff said.

"Like I said. I don't care. I get canoes and he gets money. I got no need to contact him."

"Where are the last two canoes that you bought?"

"They are out in the shed being painted."

"Let's go. We need to take a look," the sheriff said with authority. The officer motioned to Glenn and Erik to join them. They got out of the sheriff's cruiser and joined the group walking to the shed.

"Sure. If there's any problem, I'm not the one you are looking for, Sheriff."

On the way to the shed Christian looked in every direction hoping to find a clue but nothing stood out.

In the shed were two canoes that had just been painted so it was impossible to see "Moon Beach Camp" or "Four Seasons Camp" on the canoes. The State of Wisconsin ID numbers had been removed.

"I'd like you to cooperate and remove paint from one of those canoes so I can see what's written on it. Do you mind?"

"No. It will clear me. I didn't see anything written on the canoes when they were delivered. If they'd had camp names on them, I'd have been suspicious. But, for all I know the guy that sold them to me bought them from a camp looking for some easy cash."

Glenn, Christian, and Erik believed the canoes belonged to them, but there was no way they could prove it.

The officer took some paint remover and was able to wipe away some of the paint where the camp name would have been.

There was no camp name on the side. Christian looked over on the work bench and saw a sander with wire brushes. He suspected that the camp names were sanded off before the canoe was painted.

"Ok, looks like you're clean. I appreciate your answering my questions."

While the group was talking, Christian walked out of the shed and went around back. There he saw a pickup and on the side was a magnetic sign, "Northern Wisconsin Used Sports Equipment."

BINGO, Christian thought. *This case is now solved.*

When the others came out of the shed, Christian asked the sheriff to join him for a moment. The others continued walking while Christian talked to the sheriff telling him what he had seen behind the shed. "I took a photo of the pickup and in the corner of the photo will be the date and time and it will show that the pickup with the sign was at the canoe livery when we were here talking to the owner."

"Great work, Christian. But, I still need a little more evidence. He could claim that the owner left it here because it had some mechanical problem and he'd come back and get it."

"Really? This isn't enough to lock him up for stealing canoes?"

"Afraid not. Nobody saw him actually take a canoe. I have no evidence that any of these canoes came from Moon Beach or Four Seasons Camp."

"I have the piece of evidence that you need," Christian said, checking his notes.

"What's that?"

"On one of these used canoes you will find the Christian symbol of a fish, one to two inches wide, on the back right side, a few inches from the top of the canoe. I have a witness who will testify that he carved the fish onto the aluminum canoe. The witness is a camper at Moon Beach Camp."

"Hmmm, that will do it. We'll have to look for that now. If we leave, this guy might get rid of the evidence claiming he sold the canoes to someone else."

The sheriff approached the owner. "I need you to put all of your used canoes in a line. I need six pieces of steel wool. We're about to find out if these canoes were stolen or not."

"I don't get it."

"Just get some steel wool and line up the used canoes."

The sheriff told each person to sit in the back of a canoe. Then he told them to reach over the right side of the canoe, and using a pad of steel wool to get rid of the paint, rub the area down to the aluminum while looking for an etching of a fish.

All five sat in the back of five canoes, rubbing like mad when all of a sudden Erik said, "I win! Here is a fish!"

"As I said, Sheriff," Christian replied.

"You are under arrest for stealing canoes, mister," the sheriff said with authority.

"Hey, what's going on here?"

"The pickup behind the shed, the etched fish on this canoe is enough for me to convince a prosecutor that you're the canoe thief."

The man looked down at the ground and allowed the sheriff to put on the handcuffs and to put him in his car. The sheriff told Glenn and Erik to wait and he'd send a deputy out to get them. He wanted Christian to go with him to help with paperwork.

Glenn put his arm around Christian, "Good job, son. I'm very proud of you. You did a marvelous job of investigating this."

"Thanks, Dad."

"Now all I have to do is write this up and I'll have my first case solved and written into a short story. This is fun. I just might make this a career, Dad."

"Writing or investigating?" Glenn asked.

"Yes and yes," Christian replied with a smile.

The End

The Mysterious Moon
Beach Monster

The Mysterious
Moon Beach Monster

Virginia Beltzer was a bit nervous about going to camp. Her sister Bryn had told her that she would have a lot of fun because she was adventurous, but she was a bit insecure and easily became homesick if not around members of her family. Virginia arrived at the entrance to Moon Beach Camp with a nervous stomach. She got out of the family car but wanted to get right back in and go home. Her mom convinced her to give this camp a chance and if after a day or two she was miserable, she could come home.

The first people Virginia met were Sophia Rose Svetnicka, her father, Glenn, the camp manager, and her mother Adele. Sophia looked forward to camper arrival day because it usually meant new friends for a week or two. The only problem was that as soon as she got to know her new friends, it would be time for them to return to cities and villages throughout the

Midwest. But, her mom assured her that some good friends for a couple of weeks were better than not meeting any new kids.

Virginia and Sophia Rose hit it off wonderfully. Their personalities were perfect for becoming friends. If you stretched your imagination a bit, you might take them for twins. Both had curly, blonde hair, blue eyes, and were 10 years old.

One of the traditions of the campers was the snipe hunt. Going out to find the snipe was a way of initiating new campers to Moon Beach Camp. The anticipation began at the first campfire meeting of the new camp session. A counselor would tell the campers that a snipe had been seen in the area and they should be on the lookout for it. He told the campers that a snipe hunt may be needed later in the week. The new campers didn't know what to think of this mysterious creature.

"What's a snipe?" Virginia asked Sophia Rose the next morning at breakfast.

"There's no such thing," Sophia replied, shaking her head.

"Somebody just made it up?"

"Yeah, I'm not supposed to tell anyone about it, but I like you, and it's sort of stupid. Don't worry about the snipe hunt. The older kids will make it up to be scary and then on Thursday, after dark, everyone goes off into the woods looking for this snipe."

"It sounds kind of spooky."

"Yeah, the older campers are hiding in the woods and when a snipe hunter comes along they make animal sounds."

"It sounds scary."

"It can be, but that's the idea to scare the new campers."

"I'll bet it does." Virginia replied. "I'd be terrified out in the woods at night, hearing all those sounds."

"Yeah, if you fall for it, it's a scary night. But when it's over the new campers are told that they are now officially Moon

Beach Campers, and they are sworn never to tell a new camper about the snipe hunt."

"Thanks for telling me. I wouldn't have liked it."

"I figured. Just play along. But, don't tell anyone I let the snipe out of the bag. OK?"

"Oh, I won't."

"Thanks."

"Want to have some fun?" Virginia asked, with a bit of mischievous snickering.

"Sure. What are you thinking?"

"Let's create a snipe," Virginia said with a huge smile on her face.

"Create a snipe?" Sophia Rose replied.

"Sure. If one doesn't exist, we can create a snipe and really have some fun."

"I'll have to ask my dad," Sophia said, a bit skeptical of what Virginia was thinking. "He's in charge of the camp and he needs to know. We can't do anything without his approval."

"**S**ounds like fun, Sophia," Glenn said. "What have you and Virginia got in mind?"

"We thought we'd make some big tracks in a muddy part of the trail."

"Sort of like Big Foot?"

"Yeah, I guess so, whoever Big Foot is."

"He's kind of a mythical character with big feet."

"I figured that, Dad," Sophia said not appreciating her father's flippant response to her question. "Is this 'Big Foot' a person or an animal?"

"Don't know, nobody has ever caught him or it. I think people see Big Foot as a huge hairy animal."

"Sort of like a bear?" Sophia asked.

"Yeah, but he walks upright, sort of hunched over a bit, and the footprints look human."

"We thought we'd make some prints for this snipe; I suppose we could also give a report of what it might look like."

"You and Virginia have fun. I'll go along with it and help you."

"Thanks, Dad."

"**W**e've got Dad's okay," Sophia Rose reported to Virginia as she was waiting for her group's turn at swimming.

"Great. We'll have our snipe hunt Wednesday night. OK?"

"Sure."

Virginia went swimming and Sophia Rose walked to the lodge. She found some paper and crayons and began to draw her idea of a snipe. She drew a set of strange feet. Her first drawings were of huge webbed feet like a duck. Then she drew some feet that looked like a chicken. Her efforts all looked like real animal tracks.

When Virginia got back from swimming, she joined Sophia Rose and they continued to create their version of a snipe. "Let's give it nine toes!" Virginia said. "No animal has nine toes."

"Ok, I'll go to the craft cabin and see if I can find some wood. Then, we'll tie nine sticks on the bottom. We'll attach it to a broom handle and then we can push it into mud like putting a cookie cutter into dough and we'll have snipe tracks."

"Cool, Sophia Rose! We're going to have fun. More fun than they will have on that scary snipe hunt Thursday night."

"We need to spread a rumor that we've seen this snipe and we need to agree on what it looks like."

"How about a creature that looks like Big Bird on Sesame Street?" Virginia suggested.

"Yeah, we could do that. Or, we could make it out to be a camel, with a huge hump, but with a head like a bear with no neck."

"Yeah, that's it," Virginia replied. "OK, so our snipe will be a huge camel with a bear head and he walks on four legs with each foot having nine toes. This is fun. When do we start this rumor?"

"I've got to talk to my dad and be sure he is okay with this. He might not allow kids to go out into the woods at night if campers think that some huge deadly animal is out there. If he agrees, we start to spread the rumor at campfire tonight. I'll come running up in the middle of a song and tell everyone I saw this huge animal. It was really scary."

"Cool! This camp is fun. You are fun, Sophia. I'm glad you are my friend."

"Me too. Here's what we'll do. Again if Dad is okay with our plan, I'll ask him to announce at breakfast tomorrow that as soon as it becomes dark, all will take flashlights and go looking for this huge animal. By then we will have planted our snipe footprints near the trails."

"Does your dad have a tape recorder?" Virginia asked.

"Yeah. Why?" Sophia Rose asked.

"We could record a spooky sound and when the campers come along, we can turn on the recorder and really scare them."

"We can do that. Great idea!"

The campfire was aglow on a night when the full moon was shining bright in the northern Wisconsin sky. The campers were singing the last song when Sophia Rose came running to the group. "Help! Help!, HELP!" shouted Sophia Rose, panting and throwing herself on the ground, exhausted.

"What's the matter?" a counselor asked, getting up and going to her side. The counselors had been briefed by Glenn so they were able to play along with the joke.

"I saw this big thing in the tree," Sophia said, shaking in fear.

"Must have been a raccoon," said one of the older campers laughing.

"It wasn't a raccoon! It was huge like a bear!"

"Where did you see it?" a counselor asked.

"Back in the woods. Back there," Sophia said, pointing away from the campfire and the camp.

"What are you doing out there at this hour?" a counselor asked.

"I was looking for a snipe." All the older campers laughed.

"Looking for a snipe?"

"Yeah, I wanted to try and find it before tomorrow," Sophia explained.

"Was the animal a snipe, Sophia?" the counselor asked.

"I don't know. I've never seen a snipe before. Maybe it was."

The older, experienced campers all let out a loud laugh. "She thinks she saw a snipe!" a veteran camper roared as some older campers joined the laughter.

"Wait till you see it," Sophia said, beginning to catch her breath. "I turned around to see it and all I could see were the branches swaying—but I know it was BIG!"

"We'll have to report this to your dad, Sophia. Are we in any danger?" the counselor asked.

"You don't want to see this thing. He could eat us in one bite!" Once again the older campers chuckled. *Sophia Rose was doing a great job. Maybe she would grow up to be an actress,* Virginia thought.

"Ok, we'll go back to the lodge now for a snack and then to cabins for the night," the counselor said. "Stick together; we don't want to lose anyone to this monster."

"There's no monster!! That kid's just got a big imagination. She's just putting us on," an older girl shouted while others shook their heads in disbelief.

"Maybe Sophia Rose really saw something," Virginia said, standing up for her friend.

"Right! Like you believe her or something."

"Sophia Rose wouldn't make something like that up. I think there really is a monster out in the woods."

"Think what you want. The kid is nuts."

The next morning at breakfast, Glenn made his morning announcements. All were surprised to hear him say, "We've got to be on the lookout for a huge unknown animal that may be in the woods." A couple of older campers chuckled.

"This isn't funny. Some unidentified footprints have been found down at the beach and near a few paths around the camp. We've put rope around these prints so no one is to disturb them."

The older campers looked at each other and for the first time believed that maybe there was some truth to Sophia's story. The chuckling and laughter stopped.

"Tonight, instead of campfire, we will go on a hunt for this thing. We'll go in small groups and everyone must have their flashlight with them. Each group should have a camera or two in case you come upon this thing. We may need to see a photo to help us identify the mysterious animal or whatever it is. Remember, do not disturb the strange footprints inside the roped off areas. Have fun today. There is no reason to be concerned or afraid. But, we've got to figure out what this thing is. Tonight, gather at the lodge at 9:30 for the hunt."

Needless to say, the campers talked all day about the possibility of a huge animal living out in the woods. They all looked at the footprints with the nine toes and all agreed that it looked real. At 9:30 all the campers were in warm jackets and caps. Each camper had a flashlight and many had cameras. There was an air of excitement and a little fear among the campers as they remembered Sophia Rose running into the songfest at the campfire last evening all scared and exhausted.

Glenn welcomed them. "May I have your attention please. I have met with the counselors and directed them to keep all of you in their sight at all times. We will use the buddy system that we use at swimming. Each of you will be responsible for another. If you encounter anything strange, tell your counselor immediately. Your safety is very important. This hunt will only last one half hour. Pizza and pop will be waiting for you here in the lodge. Any questions? OK, let's go and fan out—your counselor knows the area you are to search."

All the campers walked together with flashlights pointing in all directions. If there were a mysterious being in the woods, he'd have lots of company within the next half hour.

The campers did not realize that Sophia Rose and Virginia were not with them. The campers in Virginia's cabin had been told that she was in the infirmary, not feeling very well. While the campers were being briefed, Adele was having a talk with the two ten-year-olds.

"I know you are having a lot of fun, but I want you to know that all that you are doing is dishonest. You do realize this, don't you?"

"We're just having fun and Daddy said it was okay," Sophia said seriously.

"I know you're having fun, but you must also know that you're spreading a lot of untruths and that is serious business."

"You mean we're lying, don't you, Mrs. Svetnicka?" Virginia said.

"That's right."

"Ah, Mom, we're just doing to others what was going to happen tomorrow night at the snipe hunt. What's the difference?"

"I know it's a joke, but sometimes a joke can be harmful."

"How can that be?" Sophia asked.

"Well, you scared some kids. You have some thinking there is a monster out in the woods." The two girls looked at each other and giggled. Their plan was working. "The nurse told me that some kids came to her saying they were sick and then admitted that they were scared of the monster."

"We're just having a little fun."

"Well, they are believing you and taking you at your word. The next time one of you says that you saw or heard something, you won't be believed. You get to play this joke only once because from then on no one will trust you." The two girls bowed their heads and looked at the floor.

"Mr. Svetnicka said it was okay," Virginia said.

"Yes, he did. Part of camping is having some fun and looking for something mysterious is having some fun. Your dad thought it was time to turn the tables so to speak on the older campers. He thinks there is some satisfaction in giving them a joke as well."

"We think so, too!" Sophia Rose said, flashing a huge smile while Virginia giggled.

"You need to go on with your practical joke, but just know that telling lies is not a good idea, and when you do, there's often a price to pay. Do you understand?"

"Yes, Mom."

"Yes, Mrs. Svetnicka."

The two girls went off with their flashlights to await the campers so they could turn on the recorder and watch the campers scream when they heard the bloodcurdling sounds from the recorder.

The groups looked and looked but found nothing. There were many scared campers once they heard the sounds. A half hour later the campers converged at the lodge and before the pizza and pop were brought out, Glenn addressed all the campers. "Thanks for looking for this monster. We didn't find him tonight but I think he's still out there waiting to scare our campers. So, I am forbidding anyone from going into the woods. Oh, and by the way, the snipe hunt scheduled for tomorrow night is cancelled. We can't take any chances with losing a camper to the belly of a monster!"

The campers looked at each other with great concern. While they had not seen the monster they had seen footprints and heard a sound that was undoubtedly coming from some being in the woods. And, if you can't trust the daughter of the camp manager, Sophia Rose, who can you trust. After seeing the footprints, most thought that Sophia was telling the truth about being chased by a strange and huge monster.

"Do you have anything to say, Sophia?" Glenn asked.

"Virginia and I want to thank all of you for looking for the monster of Moon Beach Camp. I guess we need to be honest and tell you that there is no monster of Moon Beach Camp. We played a practical joke on all of you."

The campers looked at each other in disbelief. Some chuckled. Some laughed. Some gave Virginia and Sophia Rose thumbs up. Some booed. Everyone reacted in some way.

"Scaring new campers with a snipe hunt needed a change," Sophia said. "Virginia and I decided to give all of you a hunt unlike any other. Consider yourself sniped at Moon Beach Camp!"

"Pizza and pop is served!" Glenn said as Loretta, the camp cook, brought in several pizzas. Everyone took a slice and talked about Sophia and Virginia's practical joke.

One of the older campers stood up and got everyone's attention. "Well, looks like we all fell for this thing. It was a good joke and you two need to be praised for your creativity. You had us all believing there was a mysterious something or other near the camp." Sophia and Virginia smiled at each other and gave each other high fives.

"We all got together and got you something to thank you for telling us about this monster. We planned to give it to you at campfire. It's in a bag on a log by the fire pit. Since Mr. Svetnicka says we are not to go out there, we suggest you two go and get it." Everyone clapped and cheered. Sophia Rose and Virginia bowed and waved to all the campers.

The two went out the front door of the lodge and headed for the campfire area. On their way they talked about how successful their practical joke had been. As they approached the fire pit they could see the paper bag on the log.

"What do you think they are giving us?" Sophia Rose asked.

"I think it is a snipe!" Virginia exclaimed with a laugh.

They shined their flashlights on the bag and opened it when

all of a sudden...out from a grove of trees jumped a huge bear that walked along toward the fire pit. The girls gasped and pointed their flashlights on the beast. Then it stood up on hind legs and waved with the right paw.

Virginia looked at Sophia Rose in shock and both girls ran screaming toward the lodge. They didn't stop once and burst into the building. When they entered all were laughing and clapping. "Did you find a snipe or maybe a monster or maybe a bear?" a counselor said.

"Where's my dad?" Sophia Rose asked, all out of breath.

"You won't believe what we saw!" Virginia exclaimed.

"Would you believe your mom, Sophia?"

"No way. Where is Mom? Mom? Dad?"

Adele Svetnicka came into the lodge with her bear outfit on and holding the head. All clapped and laughed.

Sophia Rose and Virginia put their hands on their hips and shook their heads. "Guess the joke is on us!" Sophia Rose said. Virginia agreed and started to laugh out of relief more than being the brunt of a joke.

"Did all of you know there was no Moon Beach Monster?" Virginia asked.

"Yup, we're pretty smart when it comes to camp jokes," one of the older campers said. "We went along with your monster hunt, but we needed to have the last word."

"You mean, 'the last monster' don't you," Sophia Rose said.

Loretta came into the dining area with a decorated cake and on it was written, "The Great Snipe Hunters!"

As everyone ate a piece of cake, Adele used the opportunity

to talk about the lesson they had just learned about being honest and not willingly deceiving others. The evening ended with Glenn's group prayer for thankfulness for Moon Beach Camp, for humor, and everyone's safety.

The End

The Case of the Missing Chocolate Chips

The Case of the Missing Chocolate Chips

Luciano Svetnicka, the 8-year-old son of camp manager Glenn Svetnicka and his wife Adele, was accused of taking a bag of chocolate chips from the kitchen storage area. The camp cook, Loretta, was used to chasing hungry boys and girls of all ages from the food storage area. She thought Luciano was the guilty one because he'd taken chocolate chips in the past.

Loretta had reported to Glenn that she had purchased 30 bags of Nestlé's® Chocolate Chips so she could make cookies for the campers. She always liked having the chocolate chips available in case a counselor or Glenn requested a batch of cookies for some special occasion. And she always kept an accurate account of all supplies.

"Mom, I didn't do it!" Luciano exclaimed when he heard that he had been accused of being the culprit.

"Good. I'm glad to hear it. But, somebody did, and you've been guilty before," his mother replied.

"It wasn't me."

"How are you going to prove it?" Adele asked.

"I'll think about it." Luciano looked depressed, worried, and innocent.

"Luciano. I believe you. I'll help you solve it," Adele said, wanting to lend a hand.

"Thanks, Mom. What do we do first?"

"Well, the first thing is to tell me your problem," Adele advised.

"Loretta said I took chocolate chips and I didn't."

"So, we've got the problem. Good. That's the first step."

"Now what?" Luciano asked.

"Well, every mystery has suspects and clues."

"What's a suspect?"

"A suspect is someone who might have taken the chocolate chips. Lorettta says you are a suspect - she thinks you took them. Who do you think took them?"

"Hmmm, I don't know. It could have been anybody."

"Could it have been your dad, sister, brother, or me?" Adele asked.

"I don't think so," Luciano replied shaking his head left to right.

"How about a counselor?"

"Maybe, but I don't think so."

"A camper?"

"Yeah, probably. Some kid probably took them."

"So, your suspect would be any camper?"

"Yeah."

"Could an animal have taken them?"

"No. I don't think so," Luciano said with a chuckle.

"So your suspect is a camper. Now, any clues?"

"What's a clue?" Luciano asked.

"A clue is something that you find that makes you think somebody took the chocolate chips. If you found an empty bag in a cabin trash can—you would have a clue that maybe the thief is someone in the cabin. But, you need to be careful, because the real thief may have put the empty bag there to throw you off."

"Solving crime isn't easy, Mom."

"No, it isn't. But you can do it. You need to look for clues."

"Maybe I should try and find an empty bag."

"That's a good place to start. You could walk all over camp, looking in trash cans. You might look under beds; just keep your eyes open wherever you go."

"OK."

"Don't open anything that is not yours. Don't open anyone's luggage or drawer or backpack. That is private property. Understand?"

"Yeah, just look around, but be sure to look in trash cans, or any place the thief could have thrown the bag away."

"Right. Come back and let me know if you find an empty bag of chips or even if you find a bag with chips in it. No camper should have a large bag of chips. If they do, you might have solved your mystery."

"See you, Mom."

Luciano walked all over the camp. He looked in every trash can. He went into the crafts cabin, into the lodge, and he walked into every boy's bathroom to look around. He didn't find an empty bag.

As Luciano was walking toward his home, known to all as The White House, to tell his mom that he had not found a bag, he looked to his right and saw a large red cross. Infirmary! Maybe someone is sick from eating a whole bag of chocolate chips? Luciano thought. He walked into the Eagle Cabin and talked to the nurse, Jane.

"Hi, anybody sick in here?" Luciano asked.

"Yes, I've got three at the moment," Jane said.

"What's wrong with them?"

"One is homesick and wants to call her mother. Another has a stomachache and might be sick to his stomach. The third got a bee sting and I'm watching to see if a rash develops."

"Who has the stomach ache?" Luciano asked.

"Some man who is visiting."

"You mean a Mom or Dad of a camper?"

"I don't think so," Jane replied. "He looks like a grandfather to me."

"What's his name?" Luciano asked.

"I don't know," the nurse replied.

"Thanks."

Luciano left the infirmary and headed for home. He decided to look around the waterfront. When he got to the canoes, he looked down and there was a chocolate chip. He glanced right and left and saw two more. The chips seemed to lead him into the woods. He followed the trail, but then all of a sudden the chips stopped.

The trail was heading to the campfire. Maybe the chips are under a log by the campfire, Luciano thought. He walked to the campfire and looked all around but did not find any chips or an empty bag. Disappointed, he headed for home.

"What did you find?" Adele asked.

"I didn't find a bag. I found out there's a sick man in the infirmary. I found some chips on the beach by the canoes and I followed a trail that goes to the campfire."

"Any chips at the campfire area?" Adele asked.

"Nope. I didn't see anything there."

"Sounds like you're stuck."

"That sick man is on my mind," Luciano replied.

"Who is he?"

"A visitor."

"Mr. Baldwin?" Adele asked.

"I don't know his name. Maybe. Who is Mr. Baldwin?" Luciano asked.

"He used to live across the street from us when you were a very little boy. He liked you and you would always give him a big smile when he came around."

"I don't remember him."

"You were very young."

"Why is he here?" Luciano asked.

"He writes mysteries," his mother responded. "He wanted to visit us and probably is thinking of ideas for his next book."

"He writes books?"

"Yeah. In fact, he put your name in one of his novels."

"Really? I'm in a book?" Luciano asked, surprised and flattered.

"Your name is."

"Cool!! Could he have taken the chips?" Luciano asked.

"Oh, no. He would never do anything like that. He's a very kind man. He's not a thief."

"What gave him a tummy ache, Mom?" Luciano asked.

"I don't know. It could have been something he ate at breakfast."

"I think it was a bag of chocolate chips."

"I'm sure he wouldn't eat a whole bag of candy. I know him and he'd never do that."

"He's a suspect, if that is what you call someone who may have stolen the chips," Luciano said.

"You can call Mr. Baldwin a suspect, but I think you are creating a red herring."

"What is a red herring?" Luciano asked.

"A red herring means a suspect who is not guilty but many people think he is."

"Where is Mr. Baldwin staying?"

"He's staying in the Mallard Cabin."

"Can I look for some clues in the cabin?" Luciano inquired.

"Oh no, it is his cabin," Adele replied firmly.

"He won't know. He's in the infirmary."

"Well, it isn't polite to go looking around in his room."

"I just want to look in the wastebasket."

"I guess that's OK. You can go in the cabin and look and then you come right back here."

"Thanks." Luciano went to the Mallard Cabin. The door was open. He went in and walked to the wastebasket. He looked in and there on the bottom of the basket were two empty M&M packages. Luciano lifted the empty packs from the basket. He glanced over on the dresser and there was a six-pack of Hershey candy bars. Three of the six were missing. Luciano returned to his mother.

"What did you find?"

"I found these." Luciano gave Adele the two empty packs.

"And on the dresser is a pack of chocolate candy bars and three of them are gone.

I think he's the guilty one, Mom."

"Whoa! Not so fast," Adele replied. "All we know about Mr. Baldwin is that he likes M&Ms and Hershey candy bars. Most people do, so that isn't enough to accuse him of taking chocolate chips."

"But, Mom, he likes chocolate. He has to be the thief."

"I like chocolate, you like chocolate, your dad likes chocolate. It's a popular candy. Now, if you had found an empty bag of Nestlé's® Chocolate Chips, that would be another thing, but you didn't. You have a suspect and some clues. I don't want to burst your bubble, but you don't have much evidence, son."

"Let me go back to the cabin and look in his suitcase."

"Absolutely not! That is private property."

"I'll bet the chips, if any are still not eaten, are in his suitcase."

"Then you will need a search warrant."

"What's that?"

"That's what the police have to get from a judge if they want permission to look in someone's home or car or a place that is private."

"You pretend to be the judge and I'll ask you, Mom."

"No. I won't allow it. You'll have to try and solve your case without looking in Mr. Baldwin's suitcase or anything that belongs to him."

There was a knock on the door. A camper about ten years old was standing on the porch. Adele and Luciano went to see who was there.

"Hi," said Adele. "Can we help you?"

"I'm looking for the boy who is trying to find the chocolate thief."

"That's me," Luciano said.

"I was in crafts and I saw three kids with chocolate on their hands."

"Good. Thanks for telling me."

"I don't mean to rat on them, but I don't like to see you in trouble because I don't think you took them."

"Thanks," Luciano said, happy to get a new clue. "I'll be back, Mom, I've got to check this out."

Luciano went to the crafts cabin and talked to the counselor. "Did you see any campers eating chocolate chips?"

"Cookies."

"Where did they get them?" Luciano asked.

"Gretchen's mother sent her a batch. She got them this morning at mail call."

"You're sure?"

"Yeah, I saw a couple of kids eating the cookies."

"OK, thanks."

"You still investigating the missing bag of chocolate chips, Luciano?" the crafts counselor asked.

"Yeah. I'm not guilty but I'll solve it."

"Good for you."

"You might talk to Claire, the lifeguard. I know she loves chocolate."

"OK, thanks. I will."

Luciano walked to the waterfront. *This could explain why I found chips by the rowboats. Maybe I'll solve this. Who would suspect the lifeguard?* Luciano thought.

Claire was taking a break and raking the beach when Luciano arrived. She was wearing a University of Wisconsin sweatshirt and had a whistle around her neck.

"Hi, Claire."

"Hi there. How's my little friend?"

"Fine. I'm trying to solve a mystery."

"Good for you. What's the problem?" Claire asked.

"I'm trying to find out who took a bag of chocolate chips from the kitchen storage area. I thought it could be you because you love chocolate. And, I found some chips around here this morning."

"It was not me, Luciano. I do love chocolate, but I didn't take the chocolate chips."

"OK. Do you have any idea who did?"

"I think it's the man who is visiting. I saw him eating something when he came down here this morning."

"I think it's him, too," Luciano replied. "Thanks."

Luciano went to see his dad who was talking to Charlie about removing some trees from a recent storm.

"Hi, son. Got that mystery solved yet?"

"Nope."

"Keep at it. It takes a lot of work but it's worth it to get to the truth."

"It bothers me that Loretta thinks I did it."

"I know, but you have been guilty of taking things from storage so I understand her pointing the finger at you."

"It's not fair."

"Maybe not, but that's what happens when you get a reputation," Glenn said.

"What's that mean?"

"Reputation means that you get known for something. When your brother solved the case of the missing canoes, he got the reputation for being a good detective. On the other hand, if someone takes things that don't belong to him, when something is missing, that someone has a reputation of taking things."

"So, I have a reputation of being a thief?"

"Guess so, at least with Loretta."

"I want to change that."

"You're doing the best thing, son. If you solve it, your reputation will change and that will be good."

"Dad, I think Mr. Baldwin took the chocolate chips."

"Oh, I don't think so. That doesn't sound like something he would do."

"But, he likes chocolate."

"Almost everyone does, Luciano. Don't you?"

"Oh, yeah. But, Mr. Baldwin is in the infirmary."

"I haven't heard that."

"Yeah, Jane said he has a bad stomach ache and I think it's because he ate a bag of chocolate chips."

"I suppose it's possible, but I don't think so."

"Was I in bed when he arrived?"

"I think so. He got in last evening."

"What did you tell him when he arrived?" Luciano asked.

"Tell him? Let's see. I welcomed him to Moon Beach Camp. I told him to make himself at home and to consider Moon Beach his home away from home. I always say that to our guests."

"So, if he eats a bag of chocolate chips at home, you invited him to do that here?"

"I suppose so, but Mr. Baldwin wouldn't eat a bag of chocolate chips. I'm very certain of that."

"Can I call Mrs. Baldwin?" Luciano asked.

"Why?"

"I just want to talk to her."

"Do you remember her?" Glenn asked. "Mrs. Baldwin's name is Patty. You were very young when she lived across the street in Michigan."

"I don't remember her."

"I didn't think you would. I guess you can call. Let me get my cell phone and her number."

Luciano called Mrs. Baldwin and thankfully she was at home.

"Hello."

"Mrs. Baldwin?"

"Yes."

"This is Luciano Svetnicka. I'm calling from Moon Beach Camp in Wisconsin."

"Oh, my goodness. How are you doing?"

"Fine."

"I want to ask you if Mr. Baldwin eats Nestlé's Chocolate Chips?"

Patty laughed. "Boy, does he! I have to hide them in the house so they will be there when I want to make cookies. He loves those chips!"

"If he finds them, does he eat the whole bag?"

"Yes. But he doesn't eat the whole bag at one time. It usually takes a couple of days."

"Does he like M&M's too?"

"Oh, yes. Plain or peanut."

"How about Hershey bars?"

"Yup, Big Block is his favorite if he can get that. Otherwise, plain bars will do."

"I guess Mr. Baldwin likes chocolate."

"He sure does. He likes writing mysteries and chocolate."

"I like solving mysteries and chocolate," Luciano said with a smile.

"You two have a lot in common, I think."

"I guess so. Here is my dad. Goodbye."

"Bye, Luciano. Say 'Hi' to your mom, Sophia and Christian for me."

"OK, here's my dad."

While Glenn talked to Patty, Luciano went home to talk to his mother.

"Mom, I'm pretty sure that Mr. Baldwin is the one who took the chips."

"Really? Let me hear your proof."

"Well, he likes chocolate. Claire said she saw him at the waterfront and he was eating something, and I found chips on the ground near the canoes. Finally, he has a stomachache and is in the infirmary."

"Good, but all of that is circumstantial evidence."

"Circum what?"

"Circumstantial. That means that you don't have any evidence that is strong enough to be certain that Mr. Baldwin took the chocolate chips. For example, nobody saw him. You don't have an empty bag with his fingerprints on it. You need something substantial, something that makes it clear that Mr. Baldwin is the thief."

"How about this. Dad told him to make himself at home. At home, he looks for chips where Mrs. Baldwin has hidden them. So, if he thinks this is his home, he'd go searching for chocolate chips and then eat them."

"Now you've got something! Good for you," Adele asked. "You talked to Mrs. Baldwin?"

"Yes. She says 'hi.'"

"Dad let you call?"

"Yup."

"Well, now I think you have enough evidence so that you can talk to Mr. Baldwin and see what he says."

"Let's go to the infirmary, Mom."

"Ok, let me put a stamp on this letter to Grandma and Grandpa DiNatali so I can take it to the lodge for mailing."

Luciano and Adele walked to the infirmary. "I still can't believe that Mr. Baldwin would do this," Adele said, shaking her head. "I hope you're wrong."

"I think it's him, Mom. I really do."

The two walked into the infirmary and greeted Jane.

"We're here to talk to Mr. Baldwin," Luciano said.

"He's on a cot back in room number three. You can go right in."

"Thanks," Luciano said.

When the two entered, Mr. Baldwin was lying on his cot and sleeping. Over a chair was his coat. Luciano could see the corner of the yellow Nestlé's bag sticking out. "Look, Mom. More evidence."

"Yes, I guess it is."

Mr. Baldwin awoke and groaned. "Oh, my stomach." He noticed that he had a couple of visitors. "Oh, hi, Adele and Luciano."

"Hi. Sorry you aren't well," Adele said, sympathetically.

"Thanks, my stomach is a bit upset. Jane is taking good care of me."

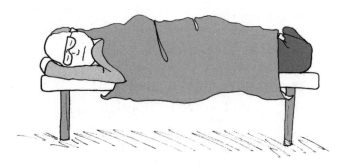

"Why do you have an upset stomach?" Luciano asked, with notebook and pencil in hand.

"I think I overdid it with some chocolate. I love the stuff, but sometimes it disagrees with me."

"You like M&M's and Hershey's?" Luciano asked.

"Oh, yeah. I sure do."

"How about Nestlé's® Chocolate Chips?"

"Oh, they're wonderful. I eat those right out of the bag!"

"Did you find some in the kitchen storage area?"

"Yes. Glenn told me to make myself at home and I guess I took him at his word. I'm sorry I if took advantage of Glenn's hospitality."

"You can have anything at our camp," Adele said. "But, let me introduce you to our newest detective. He solved The Case of the Missing Chocolate Chips all on his own."

"Solved what? Do we have a crime at the camp?" Mr. Baldwin asked.

"Loretta, our cook accused Luciano of stealing the chocolate chips," Adele explained. "He had to find the real thief to prove he was innocent."

"Thief? I'm a thief?" Mr. Baldwin asked, a bit astonished.

"Oh no, you're our guest," Adele said. "There's been a miscommunication is all."

"I didn't think the cook would miss one bag of chips and I didn't intend to keep this a secret," Mr. Baldwin explained. "I was going to pay you for them or replace them. Please, I am addicted to chocolate, but I don't think I am a thief."

"So you did take them from the kitchen storage. Right?" Luciano asked.

"Yes, I borrowed them is the way I would put it."

"I solved it, Mom! I solved it!!" Luciano said, jumping up and down.

"Yes, you did, son. Congratulations!"

70

The Case of the Missing Chocolate Chips

Mr. Baldwin shook Luciano's hand and gave him a pat on the back. "I'm proud of you, too, Luciano. Tell you what, I'll write the story of your first detective work. What's the title of your story?

"The Case of the Missing Chocolate Chips."

"Ok, I'll write it before I go back to Michigan."

"Thanks!"

The End

Moon Beach Mysteries Order Form

I really enjoyed this book and want to order more. Please send my order of *Moon Beach Mysteries* to

Name_____

Address_____

City/State/ZIP_____

	Qty.	Amount
Moon Beach Mysteries (2003) @ $6.95*		
Shipping & Handling @ $2.00		
TOTAL AMOUNT ENCLOSED		

*A 20% discount is available when 5 or more copies of Moon Beach Mysteries are purchased. Buttonwood Press will pay S&H costs beyond the $2.00 requested per order.

Please send payment by CHECK or MONEY ORDER to:

Buttonwood Press, LLC
P.O. Box 716
Haslett, Michigan 48840

Check out our website for Michigan mysteries at
www.buttonwoodpress.com